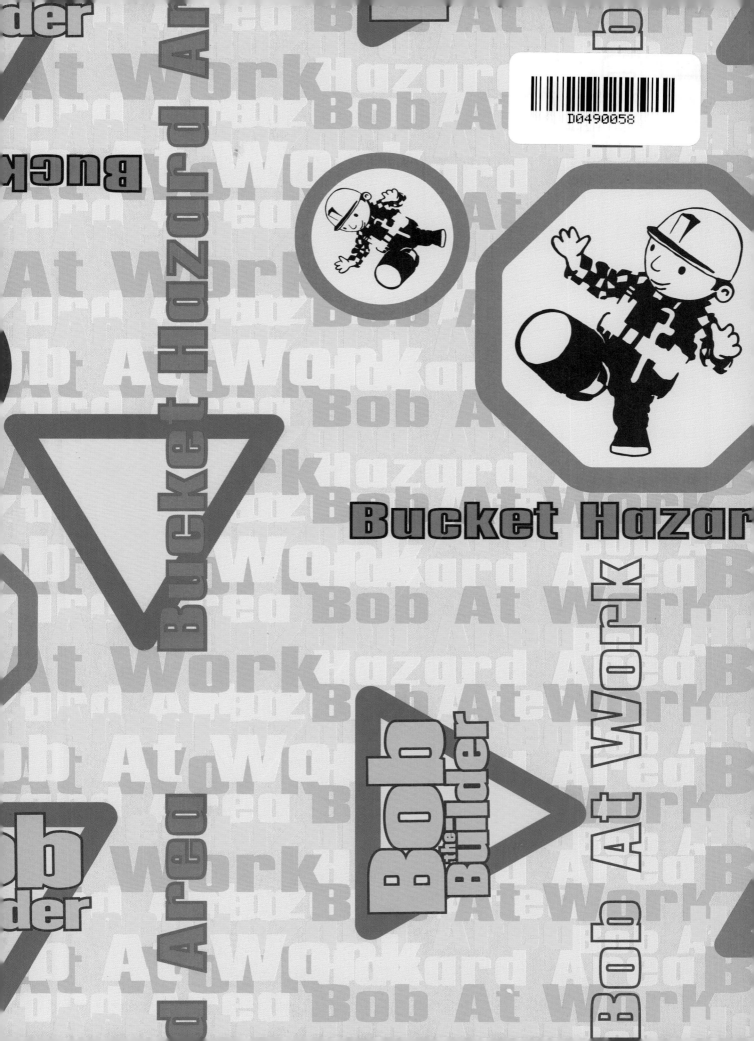

This Bob the Builder Annual belongs to

◁-----------------------------

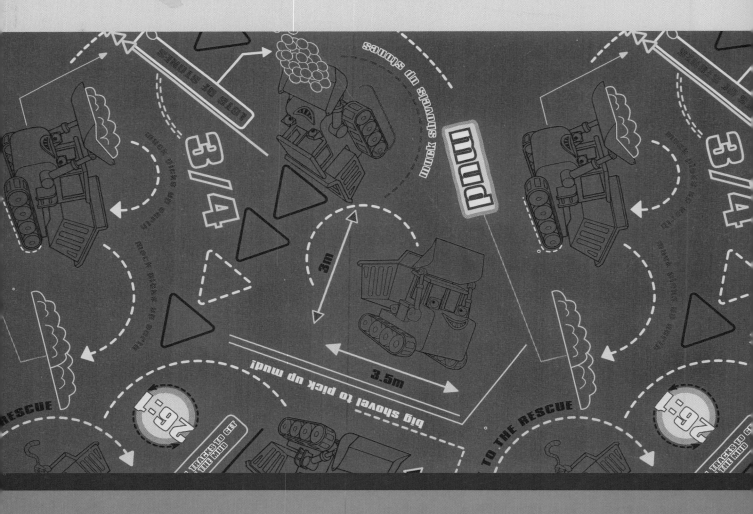

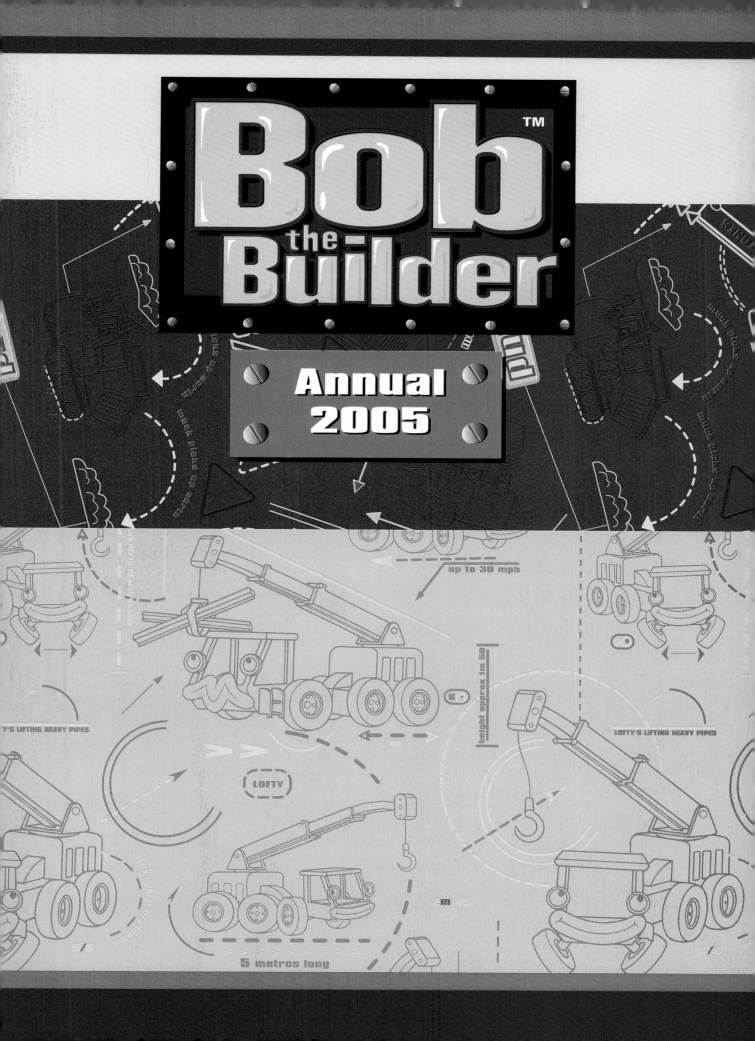

Contents

Written and edited by Brenda Apsley.   **Designed by Sally Metcalfe.**

Stories adapted from original scripts by Sarah Ball, Glenn Dakin, James Henry,
Jimmy Hibbert, Julie Jones and Diane Redmond

Based upon the television series Bob the Builder © HIT Entertainment PLC
and Keith Chapman 2004
With thanks to HOT Animation

Text and illustrations © HIT Entertainment PLC, 2004

Published in Great Britain 2004 by Egmont Books Limited,
239 Kensington High Street, London W8 6SA

Printed in Italy   3 5 7 9 10 8 6 4   ISBN 1 4052 1393 0

Bob's photo album

I got a new camera for my birthday this year. I got a photo album, too. Here are some of the photos I took of my friends at the **building yard**.

This is my favourite photo of **Wendy,** my partner in the building yard.

I called my cat **Pilchard** because she just loves eating fish – but not my goldfish, **Finn**!

This is the leader of my machine team. He's a big yellow digger called **Scoop**.

I took this photo of **Dizzy** the cement mixer when she was dancing around, as usual!

Roley the green steamroller loves music. He often sings when we're out on a job. His best friend **Bird** likes singing, too.

Don't you think **Lofty**, the mobile crane, has a lovely smile?

I like this photo of **Muck**, the digger-dumper, because he looks so happy!

Who do you think took this photo of **me**? Yes, it was Pilchard!

This space is for a picture of another of my friends – **you**!

I took all these photos at **Farmer Pickles' farm** on my day off. It was fun!

This is my good friend, **Farmer Pickles,** and his tractor, **Travis**.

As soon as he saw my camera, **Spud** the scarecrow started pulling faces and doing silly things. Look at him! He just loves messing about!

I told **Scruffty**, Farmer Pickles' dog, to say CHEESE, but he said, **"Ruff!"** instead. He always does! He's very proud of his bones, so I took some of these photos to remind him of his favourites.

Squawk is one of the black crows Spud is supposed to scare away from Farmer Pickles' fields.

I always take my camera
with me when I'm out and about.
I took these photos at **JJ's yard**.

I see a lot of **JJ** because I buy
all the things I need from his
building yard. He's always
pleased to see me.

JJ's daughter is called
Molly. I can't decide
which of these photos
of her I like best!

Skip helps Molly with the skips. They make a good team.

JJ's forklift truck, **Trix**, is always on the go. I just managed to get this photo of her and JJ before she zoomed off again.

JJ and Molly have a parrot called **Hamish**. When I said, "Would you like your photo taken?" Hamish said, **"Photo taken? Photo taken? Photo taken?"** so I took three shots!

Racing Muck

Bob and the team had an important job to do. They were going to build a new swimming pool.

"There's a lot to do," said Bob. "Dizzy, you mix some cement. Scoop, you start clearing the site."

"What can I do?" asked Muck.

"Will you go to JJ's and pick up the special tiles I ordered?" said Bob. "But be careful with them,

Muck, because they break easily."

"I'll be careful," said Muck, zooming off.

When Muck got to JJ's, Trix put the tiles into Muck's dumper, and he set off back to the site.

He remembered what Bob had said. "Must be careful," he said to himself. "Must be careful, must be careful with the ..."

Just then, Spud leapt out, waving his arms. "Stop!"

Muck stopped just in time. "You shouldn't jump out like that!" he said.

"Sorry," said Spud, "but I need a lift. I'm late, and Farmer Pickles will wonder where I am, and I'll miss my dinner and ..."

"Oh, all right then," said Muck. "Bob's waiting for the tiles, but ..."

"Great!" said Spud. "Let's go!"

Muck gave Spud a lift to his field, then he looked around. "How do I get back to the site?" he asked.

"Easy," said Spud. "You go left, then right, then left again."

"Right," said Muck.

"No, **left**," said Spud. "Look, just go straight across this field and you'll get there really quickly."

"Brilliant!" said Muck, and he zoomed off across the field.

But it was rough and bumpy, **very** rough and bumpy!

Bump! bump! went Muck's dumper, and **crack! crack!** went the tiles!

Oh, dear!

When he got back to the site, Muck said, "I found this brilliant short-cut across a field!"

"Er, was it a bumpy field?" asked Bob, unloading the tiles.

"Yeah," said Muck. "But I got back really fast!"

"A bit too fast," said Bob. "Look, the tiles are all broken."

"Oh, no!" said Muck. "Oh, I'm really sorry, Bob."

"Don't worry," said Bob. "I'll ask JJ to send Trix with some more."

Later, when Muck told Trix what had happened, she had an idea. "Can Muck come back to JJ's, Bob?" she asked. "We'll teach him how not to break things."

"Go on then!" said Bob.

Trix set out some cones in JJ's yard, and Muck weaved in and out of them, this way and that, balancing a pipe on his scoop. Then he did it wearing a blindfold, with a pile of tiles!

"I made it!" he said. "And I didn't break anything. Now I'd better get back to the site."

Later, Muck was filling a skip with rubble when Scoop noticed some broken pieces of pottery in his digger.

"Oh, no," said Muck, "I've broken something else!"

Bob looked at the pieces.

"These bits of pottery are very old," he said. "They were broken a long time before you dug them up, Muck. I think I need to make a phone call ..."

Not long after, Mr Stephens, an archaeologist, arrived at the site.

"Er, what's an arky ... oly ... thingy?" asked Muck.

"An ARK-E-OL-O-JIST is someone who looks at old things to find out how people lived a long time ago," said Bob.

"Wow!" said Muck.

Mr Stephens was looking at the pieces of pottery when Mr Bentley arrived.

"Look, flagstones, Mr Bentley," said Mr Stephens. "I think this is some sort of old road!"

"Where did the road go?" asked Muck.

"Good question!" said Mr Stephens. "Do you want to help me find out?"

"Wow!" said Muck. "Can I? Yes, please!"

Muck moved the soil so that Mr Stephens could see the flagstones.

"The road goes in a circle," said Mr Stephens. "And look, here's an old wheel ... from a chariot! Muck, you've found a racetrack that was used for chariot races!"

"Wow!" said Muck.

"This is very important," said

Mr Stephens. "We need to fence the area, and build a visitors' centre, and ..."

"But what about the swimming pool?" asked Muck.

"We'll find somewhere else to build it," said Mr Bentley.

Bob and the team soon finished the work. "There's just one more thing to do," said Bob, and he put up a plaque on the visitors' centre. "It's to let everyone know that it was Muck who found the chariot track."

"Wow!" said Muck.

"Now, it seems a shame not to use the racetrack, so ..." said Mr Stephens.

"You mean we can RACE on it?" said Muck.

Mr Stephens nodded, and as soon as Muck and the others were lined up, he started the race. "One, two, three ... GO!"

I wonder who won?

Wendy's jigsaw photos

The old pottery Muck dug up isn't the only thing that's in pieces! Wendy took some photos and made them into jigsaw puzzles to remind Muck and the team of the chariot racetrack they found.

Can you help them complete the puzzles? Which pieces will complete the pictures of the chariot racetrack, and Bob with Muck's special plaque?

Bob's busy day

It's a busy day for Bob today. He has lots of jobs to do. First he puts up some new wallpaper for Mrs Bentley, then he makes a new shed for Farmer Pickles!

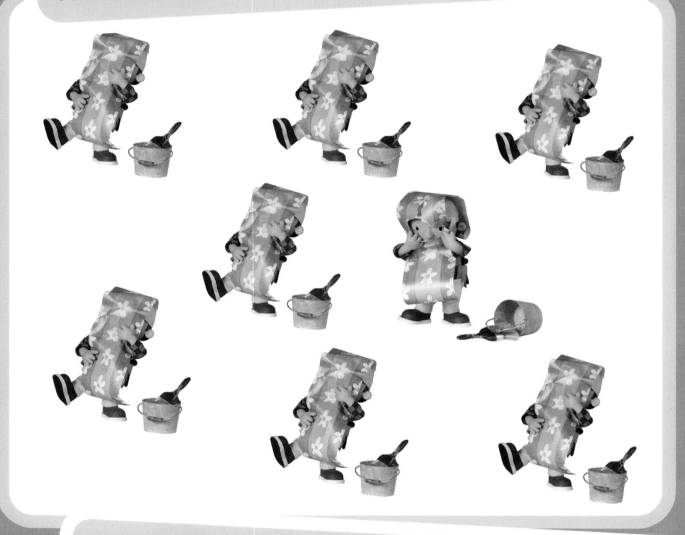

One of these pictures is different. Can you find the odd one out?

Two of the pictures of Bob are the same.
Can you find them?

Spud and the doves

1 One day, Mr Dixon took a cage with two white doves in it to Mr Ellis. He does magic tricks, and he was going to use them in his act. **"Coo, coo!"** said the doves.

2 A bit later, Spud arrived with eggs for Mr Ellis. "Coo, nice birds!" said Spud. **"Coo, coo!"** said the doves. They made Spud laugh. "Hey, I just said that! Clever birds!"

3 "Bob's building a special house called a dovecote for them," said Mr Ellis. "I'll keep them in the cage until it's ready. I don't want to leave them, but I have to go to work."

4 "I'll look after them!" said Spud. **"Coo, coo!"** said the doves. "Well, they seem to like you," said Mr Ellis, "so all right, Spud. But you mustn't let them out."

5

Spud thought the doves were really good fun. He stood on one leg, then the other – and the doves copied him! **"Coo, coo!"** said the doves. **"Coo, coo!"** said Spud.

6

Spud found Mr Ellis' magic cloak, and threw it over the cage. "Abracadabra!" he said. "Magic Spud will make the doves disappear." But they were still there.

7

Spud opened the cage. "When I say the magic word, you turn invisible," he said. "Now ... abracadabra!" – and the doves escaped!

8

Spud bowed, but then he heard a noise coming from the roof. "I've magicked you out of the cage!" he said. "Oh-oh, I'm going to be in SO much trouble!"

9

"Here, dovey-doveys!" called Spud, but the doves wouldn't go back into the cage. "Right, I'll just have to come up there and get you!" he said.

10

Spud climbed up onto the thatched roof, but his foot went through the straw. "Aaargh!" said Spud. "I'm stuck! Help!" **"Coo, coo!"** said the doves.

11

Just then, Bob and Lofty arrived to decide where to put the dovecote. "But where have the doves gone?" asked Bob. "Er, they're here," said Spud.

12

"What are you doing up there?" asked Bob. "I was trying to get the doves down, and my foot got stuck in the straw roof," said Spud. "Now I'm stuck."

13

Not for long! Lofty raised his crane arm, and put his hook under Spud's belt. Then he pulled Spud's foot free, and lowered him to the ground.

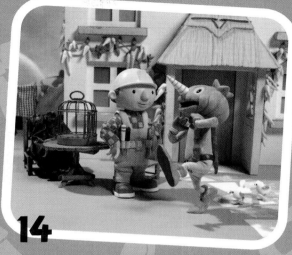

14

"I'll get the doves back into the cage," said Spud. "**Coo, coo!**" he said, moving his arms like wings. "**Coo, coo!** Come on, follow Spud the dove!"

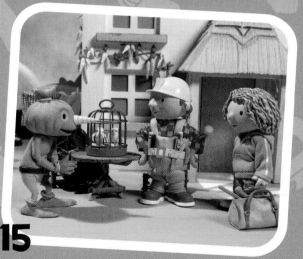

15

Spud soon got the doves back into the cage. "Can you mend the roof, Bob?" he asked. "I can't," said Bob, taking out his phone. "But I know someone who can!"

16

It didn't take Bob's friend Katie long to mend the roof. Then she showed Spud how to make a corn dolly, a good-luck model, made of straw.

17

When the dovecote was ready, Lofty and Bob took it to Mr Ellis' house. "I'll help you, Lofty!" said Spud, grabbing it by the roof.

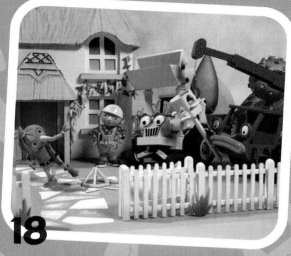

18

But the wooden roof came off in his hands! He dropped it, and it broke into pieces. "Oh, no!" said Spud. "I've done it again. Sorry, Bob."

19

"It's okay, Spud, it was an accident," said Bob, and he went off with Scoop to get some wood to fix it. As they drove off, Spud had an idea.

20

"Why don't you make a roof of **thatch** for the dovecote, Katie?" said Spud. "That's a great idea!" said Katie. "I'll do it, as long as you help me, Spud."

21

When the new roof was finished, Spud made his corn dolly while Katie and the others put up the dovecote. Then Spud put his dove-shaped corn dolly on top.

22

"That looks great, Spud," said Katie. "Really impressive!" said Dizzy. The doves seemed to like it, too. **"Coo, coo!"** they said. **"Coo, coo, coo!"**

23

When Bob and the others arrived with the wood, Katie explained that they didn't need it. "We thatched the roof instead," she told them. "It was Spud's idea."

24

Spud was so pleased that the doves liked their house that he ran round and round it, flapping his arms like wings. **"Coo, coo!"** he said. "I'm Spud the dove!"

Spud's picture pairs

I really liked Mr Ellis' two white doves. They made a neat pair! Can you draw lines to join these pictures to make pairs, and say the name of the one left over?

Molly's fashion show

One day, Molly and JJ were busy in the yard when Pam Goody came to buy some yellow paint. "It's for my office at the arts centre," she explained. "It's a bit drab and sad-looking, so I want to make it look more cheerful."

"An arts centre's supposed to be fun, isn't it?" said JJ. "Not drab and sad."

"That's right," said Pam. "And it would be a fun place, if we had enough money to finish the building work."

"We need to find a way to raise some money then," said JJ.

"What about a fashion show?" said Molly. "I could design the clothes."

"Great idea!" said Pam. "Over to you, Molly."

Molly loved the idea of a fashion show – but how was she going to set it up? "I know," she said. "I'll get Bob on the job!"

Bob and the team agreed to help Molly by building a catwalk.

"Er, what IS a catwalk, Bob?" asked Roley.

"It's a long raised platform," said Bob. "The models walk along it, so everyone can see the clothes."

"I'd love to be a model!" said Dizzy.

"You can be," said Lofty, putting a plastic sheet around her. "You can wear this!"

"Right, let's all get going," said Bob.

"No prob, Bob," said Scoop.

"**Can we fix it?**"

"**Yes we can!**" said the others.

All except Lofty. "Er ... yeah ... I think so."

Dizzy was still zooming around the yard when Spud arrived.

"Bob and Wendy are building a catwalk," said Roley.

"Coo," said Spud, "a CATwalk, eh?"

Pilchard looked up. "**Miaaaowwrr!**"

"You'll like that, won't you, Pilchard?" said Spud. "Let's go and have a look."

"**Miaaaowwrr!**" said Pilchard,

and she and Spud walked out of the yard.

"But a catwalk's not for CATS," Dizzy called out. "Oh, I'd better go after them."

● ● ●

Bob and the team got busy building the catwalk.

Scoop brought the pieces of frame, and Lofty lifted them into place so that Bob and Wendy could join them together. Wendy laid wooden boards on top, Bob fixed some steps at one end, then they made a doorway with a curtain over it.

They had just started painting when Spud and Pilchard arrived. "Time for CATwalkies, Pilchard," said Spud.

Pilchard walked through the doorway ... Bob tripped over her ... and yellow paint went everywhere, all over Bob, all over Wendy – and all over Pilchard!

"Er, I wanted Pilchard to try the

catwalk," said Spud.

Bob laughed. "But a catwalk isn't for cats! It's for models in the fashion show."

Spud liked the sound of that. "A fashion show, eh?" he said, dashing off. "See you later!"

Just then, Dizzy saw that Pilchard had put yellow paw prints on her plastic sheet. "You're getting paint all ..." she said, then stopped. "Hey, what a brilliant pattern! Oh, please do some more!"

"**Miaaaowwrr!**" said Pilchard.

• • •

At JJ's yard, Molly was trying to think of ideas for clothes. "I need something special," she said. "But what?"

"Go and have a look at the catwalk," JJ suggested. "That might give you some ideas."

Molly arrived at the arts centre just as Dizzy zoomed on to the catwalk.

"Look out, Dizzy!" said Bob. "I haven't fixed those boards yet ..."

Too late! Dizzy stepped on a loose board, and red paint flew into the air.

It landed on Molly!

"Oh, well, Molly," said Wendy. "At least you're not the only one covered in paint."

"Yes," said Molly, then she smiled. "That's it! What a great idea. See you later."

Bob and Wendy looked at each other. What was all that about?

● ● ● ●

Molly was busy all afternoon, drawing and cutting and sewing. When the clothes were ready she loaded them on to Trix.

"What about the stuff in the bin bag?" asked Trix.

"That's just some old odds and ends of fabric," said Molly. "Come on, let's go!"

When they had gone, out popped Spud. "Ooh, what have we here?" he said, looking in the bin bag. "Hee, hee, hee ..."

● ● ● ●

That night, Pam started the show. "As well as Molly, we have two other special models," she said

– and on to the catwalk walked Bob and Wendy, wearing dungarees with bright splashes of colour all over them!

"And here is Dizzy," said Pam, "modelling an outfit made by Lofty and Pilchard!"

• • •

The show was a great success. Pam was giving Molly a bunch of flowers as a 'thank you' when onto the catwalk walked Spud, in an outfit he had made from Molly's odds and ends.

"Here comes Spud the ..." he said, but he tripped on his outfit, spun around, and crashed into Bob and Wendy.

All three landed in a heap.

Molly handed a flower to Spud. "Here's Spud the scarecrow, wearing the very latest in – scarecrow wear!"

Spud posed happily as cameras flashed. "Thank you, fans!" he said. "Spud the supermodel!"

Draw with Wendy

scruffty by Wendy

Would you like to do some drawing and painting with me? Copy my picture of Scruffty piece by piece, then colour your picture. Don't forget to write your name on the line!

scruffty by _____

Travis gets lucky

You can read this story yourself. When you come to a picture, say the word.

The field mice have been eating 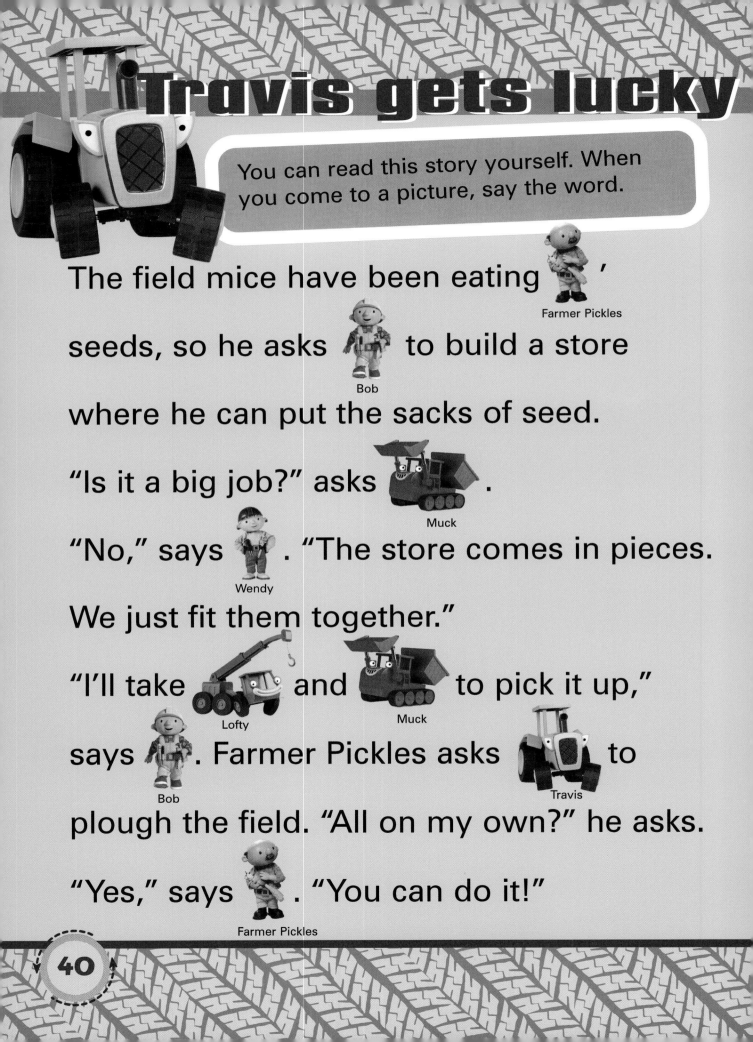 Farmer Pickles'

seeds, so he asks Bob to build a store

where he can put the sacks of seed.

"Is it a big job?" asks Muck.

"No," says Wendy. "The store comes in pieces.

We just fit them together."

"I'll take Lofty and Muck to pick it up,"

says Bob. Farmer Pickles asks Travis to

plough the field. "All on my own?" he asks.

"Yes," says Farmer Pickles. "You can do it!"

40

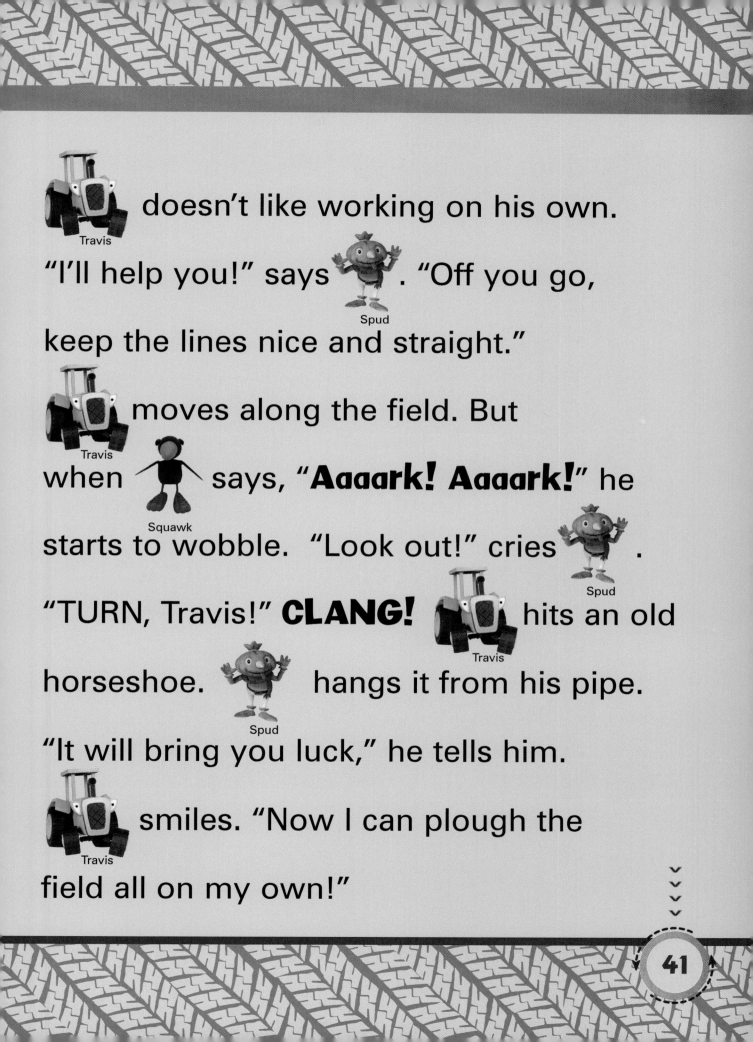 doesn't like working on his own.

"I'll help you!" says [Spud]. "Off you go, keep the lines nice and straight."

[Travis] moves along the field. But when [Squawk] says, "**Aaaark! Aaaark!**" he starts to wobble. "Look out!" cries [Spud].

"TURN, Travis!" **CLANG!** [Travis] hits an old horseshoe. [Spud] hangs it from his pipe. "It will bring you luck," he tells him.

[Travis] smiles. "Now I can plough the field all on my own!"

does really well. "It's great,"

says Dizzy. "You see, you CAN do it

on your own. I knew you could."

"My lucky horseshoe helps me," says

Travis. "Look, it's on my pipe."

But the horseshoe is not there. "Oh, no!"

says Travis. "I can't plough without it."

"Of course you can," says Bob.

"**Can he plough it?**" says Dizzy.

"**Yes he can!**" say Bob and Muck.

"Er ... yeah, I think so," says Lofty.

When  sees the field, he is very pleased.

Farmer Pickles

"I knew you could do it, ," he says.

Travis

"Well done!" As  and Wendy show

Bob

 the seed store,  runs up.

Farmer Pickles

Spud

"I found your lucky horseshoe!" he says.

"I don't need it!" says . "But YOU

Travis

might. I'm going to plant the seeds with

 tomorrow, and you'll have

Farmer Pickles

to scare  and all his friends away!"

Squawk

"**Aaaark, aaaark, aaaark, aaaark!**"

say the crows. "Oh, no!" says .

Spud

Help!

Bob is always losing his mobile phone. He often forgets where his tools are too. Can you help him find them?

Find and count Bob's tools, then write the numbers in the boxes.

Scruffty on guard

1

One day, Mr Dixon, the postman, had a parcel for Farmer Pickles. "It's a book about pigs," said Farmer Pickles. "Are they going to live on the farm?" asked Travis.

2

"That's right," said Farmer Pickles, taking out his mobile phone. "I'm going to need special homes for them called pigsties, so I'd better give Bob a call."

3

Bob and the team set off for the farm. **"Can we build it?"** said Scoop. **"Yes we can!"** said the machines. All except Lofty. "Er ... yeah ... I think so."

4

Farmer Pickles took Bob into the barn to have a look at the pigs. The daddy pig was in one pen and the mummy pig and her piglets were in another.

5

"The male pig is a bit grumpy," said Farmer Pickles. "He's called Humpty." Bob laughed. "Maybe he'll be a bit happier when he sees his new pigsty."

6

Bob got busy building the first sty. "Humpty will have his own sty, and the mother pig and her piglets will have another," said Bob. "Humpty likes to be on his own."

7

Bob was hungry, but he decided to do some more work before stopping for lunch. Scruffty wanted to see what was in Bob's lunch box! He wagged his tail: "**Ruff!**"

8

A bit later, Farmer Pickles arrived. "Have you seen my new cap?" he asked. "I put it down somewhere, and now it's gone." Bob shook his head. "No, sorry," he said.

9

"**Ruff! Ruff!**" said Scruffty, and Bob looked around. "That's funny," he said. "My lunch box is missing, too. It was here a while ago. I wonder what's going on?"

10

The team got busy again. Lofty lifted up the frame for the roof, then Bob fitted the doorways. "But the pigs can't go in until I've put up the fence tomorrow," said Bob.

11

"Okay, Bob," said Farmer Pickles. He looked around, and scratched his head. "Now what did I do with my gloves? I had them a minute ago! Where are they?"

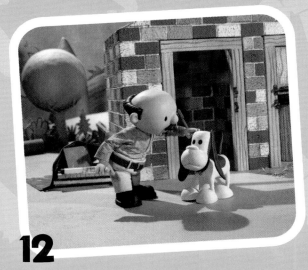

12

"A lot of things have gone missing today," said Farmer Pickles. "I'll put Scruffty on guard duty tonight. He'll keep an eye on your tools." "**Ruff! Ruff!**" said Scruffty.

13

That night, Scruffty was guarding Bob's tools when he heard a noise. **"Ruff! Ruff!"** said Scruffty. "It's me," said Spud. "I thought you might want to play."

14

"Let's play Fetch!" said Spud. He threw Bob's spirit level, and they both ran after it. Spud and Scruffty didn't know that Humpty was awake. **"Oink!"**

15

Next morning, Bob's hammer was missing! "Did you see anything, Scruffty?" asked Farmer Pickles. Scruffty hung his head and whined.

16

Spud arrived. "Did you enjoy our game last night, Scruffty?" he asked. **"Ruff!"** said Scruffty. "Did you see anyone else up here?" asked Bob. "No," said Spud.

17

"I'm sorry your tools keep going missing, Bob," said Farmer Pickles. "You know, I'm starting to wonder if my Scruffty could have anything to do with this ..."

18

Later, Spud went to say hello to the pigs. He leaned into Humpty's pen, but Farmer Pickles pulled him back. "Don't stick your nose too close," he said. "Humpty likes parsnips!"

19

The next thing to go missing was Bob's phone. Wendy had an idea. "I'll call your phone on mine, Bob," she said. "We might hear it ringing."

20

Ring, ring! "There it is," said Bob, following Scruffty into the barn. They listened. The noise was coming from Humpty's pen! **"Oink! Oink!"** said Humpty.

21

All the things that were missing were in Humpty's pen. "Well, pigs will eat anything," said Farmer Pickles. "But how did he get out?" asked Bob.

22

"Ruff! Ruff!" said Scruffty, digging away the straw that covered a hole in the wall. "Humpty's been using the hole as a door," said Farmer Pickles. **"Oink!"** said Humpty.

23

Soon the pigsties were ready, and Humpty and his family moved into their new homes. **"Oink! Oink!"** they said. "I think that means they like them!" said Bob.

24

Farmer Pickles held out a big dog biscuit. **"Oink!"** said Humpty. "It's not for you," said Farmer Pickles. "It's for Scruffty the guard dog!" **"Ruff!"** said Scruffty.

Scruffty's puzzles

Can you help Scruffty find five things that are different in picture 2?

1

2

52

Scruffty can't count very well! Can you help him? Count the number of big pigs and little piglets in the picture, and write the numbers in the boxes.

53

Mr Bentley dogsitter

One morning, Bob and the team were getting things ready for their next job when Pilchard brushed up against Bob's legs. **"Mrrrowrr!"** said Pilchard.

She was trying to tell Bob she was hungry, but Bob was so busy that he didn't notice.

"Can we fix it?" said Scoop.

"Yes we can!" said the others. All except Lofty.

"Er ... yeah ... I think so," he added, as Bob, Muck, Scoop and Dizzy left the yard.

"Rrrrrrrrrowr!" Pilchard said to Lofty and Roley.

Lofty understood. "Do you want your breakfast, Pilchard?" he asked.

"Miaow!" said Pilchard.

"Sorry, but we're too big to get into the kitchen," said Roley.

Pilchard wasn't pleased.

"MIIIAAAAOW!"

Bob and the team were making a house into two flats. Bob was telling Dizzy that there were two doors, one for the upstairs flat, and one for the downstairs one, when Mr Bentley arrived with a little dog.

"This is Timmikins," said Mr Bentley. "He's the Mayor's dog. I'm looking after him while she's on holiday."

"**Yip, yip, yip, yip!**" said Timmikins – and he leapt into Dizzy's mixer!

When Bob got him out, he was covered in concrete dust!

"Take him to the yard, Mr Bentley," said Bob. "Wendy will help you clean him up."

When he saw Lofty, Timmikins got very excited. "**Yip, yip, yip, yip!**"

"Ooo ... er," said Lofty, trying to hide in a corner. "Oh dear!"

When Wendy came out of the office, Timmikins ran over to say hello to her, too. "**Yip, yip, yip, yip!**"

"This is Timmikins, the Mayor's dog," said Mr Bentley. "He jumped into Dizzy's mixer and got rather dirty."

"I'll get some water and shampoo," said Wendy.

"Thank you, Wendy," said Mr Bentley. "Can I use your office phone?"

"Help yourself," said Wendy. She was just about to go into the house when Pilchard walked in front of her.

"**Wrrrrowr!**" said Pilchard.

"She wants some breakfast," Lofty explained, so Wendy gave Pilchard a bowl of food, then went to get the shampoo.

Pilchard was just about to eat her food when Timmikins rushed up and gulped it down, every last scrap!

"**Wrrrrroooaaar!**" said Pilchard, rushing at Timmikins.

"**Yip, yip, yip!**" said Timmikins, rushing at Pilchard.

Pilchard ran out of the yard, with Timmikins right behind her, just as Wendy and Mr Bentley came out again.

"Er, we've got a problem," said Wendy. "It's Timmikins – he's gone!"

"GONE?" said Mr Bentley. "OH, NO!"

When it was time for lunch, Bob closed both the doors of the flats and set off back to the yard. What he didn't know was that Timmikins had run into one of them, and now he was trapped inside!

When Bob got to the yard, Mr Bentley and Wendy were still looking for Timmikins. "I've got to get him back," he said. "What will the Mayor say if I can't find him? We've got to find that dog!"

"We'll find him," said Bob.

Bob and the team looked everywhere, but only one of them knew where Timmikins was – Pilchard! She went to the flats, pressed her paws on the door handle, and the door opened. Then she took his lead in her mouth, and walked him back to the yard.

"Yip! Yip! Yip! Yip!"

As soon as Timmikins saw Lofty, he rushed towards him, dragging Pilchard behind him. She trod on a button on Bob's phone, which he had dropped when he was searching the yard for Timmikins – and in the town, Wendy's phone rang.

"Hello?" said Wendy.

She heard Lofty's voice. "HELP! He's too raggy!"

Then she heard Timmikins.

"Yip! Yip! Yip! Yip!"

"It's Lofty and Timmikins," Wendy said to Mr Bentley. "They must be back at the yard. Come on!"

Timmikins was very pleased to see Mr Bentley. Timmikins gave Mr Bentley a good licking and Lofty told Wendy that it was Pilchard who had brought him back.

"Well done, Pilchard!" said Wendy.

"**Miaow!**" said Pilchard.

"You are a clever cat, Pilchard," said Bob, giving her a stroke.

"**Miaow!**" said Pilchard.

That night, Timmikins was lying on Mr Bentley's favourite chair when Mrs Bentley came in from the kitchen.

"I've got a nice piece of steak," she said.

"Oh, thank you," said Mr Bentley. "I could just eat a ... "

"But it's not for you!" said Mrs Bentley. "It's for Timmikins!"

"Oh ..." said Mr Bentley.

"**Yip! Yip! Yip! Yip!**" said Timmikins.

Bob's picture puzzle

Skip

Dizzy

Lofty

Mr Bentley

Wheel

Pilchard

Window

Travis

Look at the big picture, then look at the little pictures. How many of the little pictures can you see in the big one? Can you find and tick five?

60

1

One day, Bob and the team were going to make a new road crossing. **"Can we fix it?"** said Scoop. **"Yes we can!"** said the others. "Er ... yeah, I think so," said Lofty.

2

Mrs Percival, the school head teacher, went to see Molly. "Would you paint a jungle scene on the wall of the playground?" she asked. "I'd love to!" said Molly.

3

Later, Skip and Lofty were on their way back from the dump when they passed the school. They stopped to look at the big picture Molly was painting on the wall.

4

Lofty looked a bit worried. "Oo, er," he said. "Is that a d-dinosaur?" Molly laughed. "No Lofty, it's an elephant. Look, you can see his long trunk."

5

Lofty waved his extendable arm around, pretending to be an elephant. "Look at me!" he said. "I've got a long trunk, too. I'm Lofty the elephant!"

6

But Lofty's 'trunk' knocked over the tins of paint. "Oh, I've made a mess, haven't I?" he said. "It's okay," said Molly. "I've got some special stuff to clean it up with."

7

Molly got busy cleaning up the paint spills. She had almost finished when Mrs Percival came out to see how the big jungle picture was going.

8

"It's great!" said Mrs Percival. "But I hope you're going to paint some heads on those parrots!" Molly laughed. "Yes, it's just that I have to think of a way to reach them."

9

Molly was wondering how she could finish the parrots when she had an idea. She tied string to two empty paint tins, and used them like stilts! "Great!" said Molly.

10

Spud was delivering eggs when he saw Molly. "Why are you wearing those funny shoes?" he asked. "They're not shoes," said Molly. "Look, they're stilts!"

11

"I could deliver my eggs faster with those!" said Spud. "Can I borrow them?" Molly shook her head. "Sorry, Spud, I need them to finish the top bit of my picture."

12

When Molly finished the picture, she went to get more stuff to clean up the last bits of paint. Which is when Spud decided to borrow her stilts ...

13

When Lofty and Skip arrived to see Molly's picture, they saw the big paint-tin prints that Spud had made. "Oo ... er," said Lofty. "Look – footprints! BIG footprints!"

14

Lofty and Skip wondered what could make such big footprints. "It's an ELEPHANT!" they said. "Let's follow the footprints, and find it," said Skip.

15

When Molly got back to the school Mrs Percival showed her the messy footprints. "I don't know how they got there," said Molly. "But I'll find out!"

16

Molly followed the footprints. They led her to Spud, who was racing along on the stilts. "Aha!" said Molly. "Spud! I might have known!"

17

When Spud saw Molly he ran off. "Sorry, Molly, can't stop!" he said. "I'm in a hurry!" Molly ran after him. "Come back with my stilts!" she shouted.

18

Mr Bentley was checking the new road crossing when Spud ran across it, leaving lots of messy paint-tin prints behind him. "Oh, Spud!" said Mr Bentley.

19

Lofty used his hook to grab Spud by his pants, and he lifted him into the air. "**Whoooah!**" said Spud. "Let me down! Oh, PLEASE let me down!"

20

"You've ruined the crossing!" said Mr Bentley. "And you took my stilts without asking!" said Molly. "I'm sorry," said Spud. "I'm really sorry, honest!"

21

When Lofty put Spud down again, Skip showed him the prints the stilts had made. "They do look like elephant footprints, don't they?" he said.

22

"But there wasn't really an elephant, was there?" said Bob. "It was Spud wearing Molly's paint-tin stilts that made the footprints you followed."

23

"I never **really** thought there was an elephant," said Skip. "Neither did I," said Lofty. But they still both jumped when Molly made a funny elephant noise!

24

"Now, Spud, it's time for you to clean up all this paint," said Molly. "Oh, I wish there WAS an elephant," said Spud. "He could use his trunk to wash it all away!"

Count with Molly and Spud

There are lots of tins of paint in Molly's display! Count the number of red tins and the number of yellow tins, and write your answers in the boxes.

Now, can you count the number of footprints Spud made, and draw a circle around the correct number?

1 2 3 4 5 6 7 8 9 10